Paradise Press, Inc

Exclusive distribution by Paradise Press, Inc.
© Creation, text and illustrations: A.M. Lefèvre, M. Loiseaux,
M. Nathan-Deiller, A. Van Gool
This 1999 edition produced by ADC International, Belgium
and published by Ottenheimer Publishers, Inc.,
Owings Mills, Maryland. All rights reserved.
SCO57MLKJIHGFEDCBA

Printed in Singapore

Peter Pan

'''VAN GOOL'''

One night in London, Mr. and Mrs. Darling were putting their children, Wendy, John and Michael, to bed. Nana the dog was helping them. "Look Mummy," said Wendy, picking up some leaves, "Peter Pan has been here. I wonder where he is now?"

"He must be in Never-Never Land," cried John and Michael.

Mr. Darling smiled. "Peter Pan doesn't exist," he told them. "Now go to sleep and forget this nonsense."

Later that evening, Mrs. Darling was sewing by the nursery. Everything was very quiet, and soon she had fallen asleep. A strange noise awoke her.

"That sounded like leaves rustling," she thought.

Suddenly she saw Peter Pan flying around the room, and cried out in surprise.

Nana began barking at Peter Pan, who flew quickly out of the window. Nana couldn't catch him, but she did catch his shadow.

The next evening, Mr. Darling was trying to make Michael swallow his medicine. "Don't want it," grumbled Michael. "It will help you sleep," said Mr. Darling. "And it tastes lovely! Do it like this." He lifted a glass to his lips.

But Mr. Darling did not drink the medicine. While the children were not looking, he poured it into Nana's bowl. Mr. and Mrs. Darling were going to a party that night, and left Nana to look after the children. But the medicine made her very sleepy, and soon she was snoring gently!

Later that night Peter Pan flew to
the Darling house. It was a warm
night, and the nursery window was
open. "Now I can get my shadow
back," he whispered to the tiny
twinkling light beside him.

Peter's shadow was in the nursery, but when Peter tried to make it come with him, the shadow wouldn't leave! "Come here, you silly shadow!" cried Peter, angrily.

Peter was being so noisy that Wendy woke up. She was delighted to see him. "I'll sew your shadow back, Peter," she said. When she had finished, Peter gave Wendy a necklace to say thank you. Just then Wendy noticed the tiny light Peter had brought with him.

"Wendy, this is Tinkerbell," said Peter.

Then Peter Pan had an idea.
"Why don't you come with us to
Never-Never Land?" he asked.
"Yes please!" cried Wendy, and
she quickly woke her brothers.
"Hurry up!" she told them.
"We're going to Never-Never
Land with Peter Pan!"

Tinkerbell sprinkled the
children with pixie dust to help
them fly. Then they all flew out
of the nursery window, and over
the rooftops of London.

It was a long flight to Never-Never Land, but at last the children could see the island. Tinkerbell led the way, as it was very dark. Suddenly… WHIZZ!… A red light lit up the sky. "A cannonball!" cried Peter. "Look out, Wendy, the pirates are firing at us!" But the warning came too late.

Captain Hook, the pirate leader, was very angry. "You idiots!" he cried to his men. "You missed Peter Pan! Ever since that wretched boy cut off my hand and gave it to the crocodile, I've vowed to have my revenge, and now you've missed him!"

The pirates cowered as Captain Hook continued. "Now we must find the Lost Boys' hideaway. If we capture them, Peter Pan will have to come for them!"

The pirates began to search the island. Suddenly Captain Hook heard voices. He realized they were coming from a chimney, hidden in a mushroom. "Here they are!" he cried, "Now I'll get my revenge!"

Just then he heard another sound. Tick-tock, tick-tock, tick-tock. "It's the crocodile!" he cried and hurried back to the boat. The crocodile was always trying to eat the rest of Captain Hook. However, he had once swallowed a clock, so the pirates could always hear him coming.

Wendy was lost. She had Tinkerbell with her, but the little fairy was jealous of Wendy. "She wants to take Peter away from me," she thought. As soon as Wendy wasn't looking, Tinkerbell flew straight to the Lost Boys' camp.

"Peter wants you to shoot a big white bird in the sky," she told them. When they saw Wendy, the Lost Boys fired stones at her.

One of the rocks hit Wendy, and she fell to the ground. Just then Peter Pan returned. When he saw Wendy, he was very angry. "What have you done? Wendy was going to be a mother to look after you, and you've killed her!"

When Peter learned that it was Tinkerbell's idea, he was even more angry. "Go away, Tinkerbell," he said. I don't want to see you any more."

One of the Lost Boys suddenly pointed at Wendy, who had begun to open her eyes. "Look, she's alive!" he cried. As Wendy sat up, John and Michael walked into the camp. The Lost Boys were very happy. Now they had two new friends to play with, and a mother to look after them!

31

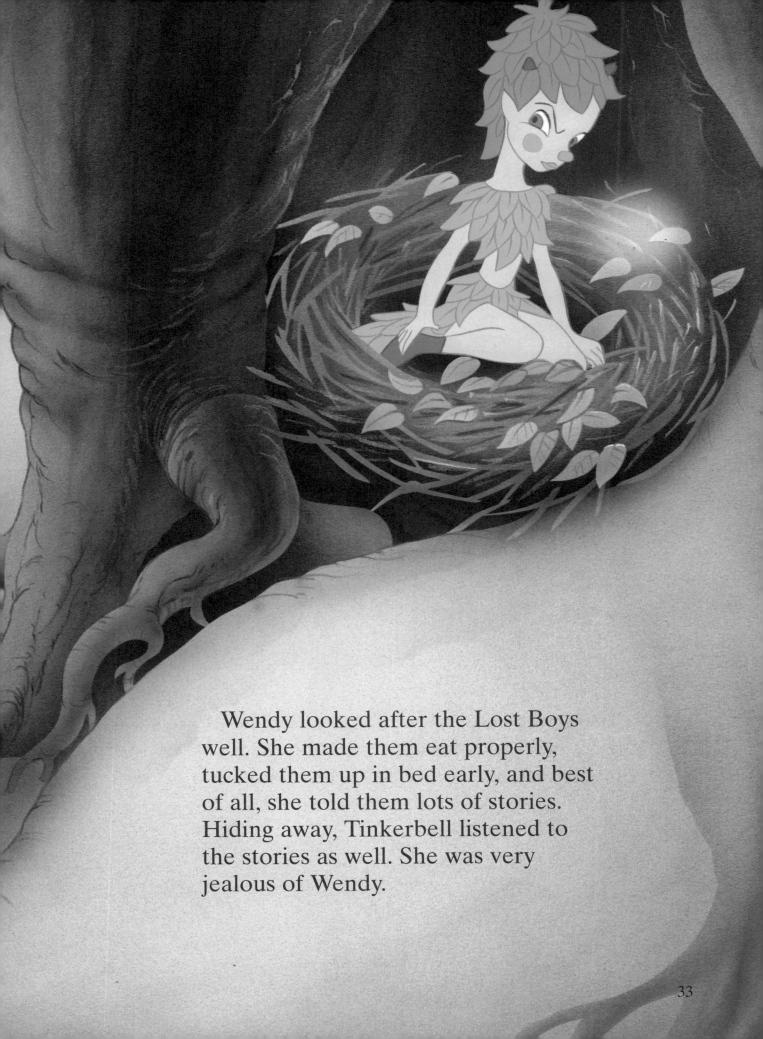

Wendy looked after the Lost Boys well. She made them eat properly, tucked them up in bed early, and best of all, she told them lots of stories. Hiding away, Tinkerbell listened to the stories as well. She was very jealous of Wendy.

33

Peter Pan showed Wendy and her brothers all around Never-Never Land. He took them to meet the mermaids, but they hated Wendy on sight. "Make her go away, Peter," they cried. "Then we can play."

Wendy was very sad that the mermaids would not speak to her. Just then Peter heard a cry for help. "That's Tiger Lily, the Indian Chief's daughter," he said. "The pirates have captured her. We must help her!"

The pirates were tying Tiger Lily to a rock. "She'll drown when the tide comes in!" gasped Wendy. Peter hid behind a boulder, and imitated Captain Hook's voice.

"Release Tiger Lily!" he called.

"But Captain," protested the pirates, "you said…"

"I've changed my mind. Now let her go!" The pirates obeyed, and untied Tiger Lily.

The real Captain Hook arrived at that moment. "Where is Tiger Lily?" he demanded.

"Hello, Hook!" said Peter Pan, appearing before him. "I've let Tiger Lily go!"

Hook was furious that Peter had spoiled another of his wicked plans. He drew his sword, and a terrible fight started.

Chasing Hook across the rocks, Peter Pan slipped and fell. He hit his head, and lay still. Then Captain Hook bashed him on the head with his hook. "The sea will soon finish him off," said Captain Hook, and strode happily back to his ship.

Wendy had been watching everything from her hiding place, and ran to Peter's side. "How are we going to get home?" she wondered. "Peter's too heavy for me to carry."

Wendy stayed by Peter as the tide slowly crept up the rocks. He woke up, but was too weak to fly. Suddenly Wendy cried out. "There's Michael's kite! That will help us get home!" She caught the string, and the kite lifted them into the air and away from the rocks.

Back at the Lost Boys' camp, Peter rested while Wendy told the Lost Boys all about her home in London. "I do miss my parents," she said. "Why don't you all come back home with us? I know my parents will look after you!" The Lost Boys were very excited but Peter Pan was sad. "I don't want to grow up," he said.

Because Peter Pan had saved Tiger Lily, the Indians were standing guard outside the Lost Boys' home. But the crafty pirates took them by surprise, and tied up all the Indian guards in the middle of the night. The next morning a pirate banged the Indians' drum, so the children thought it was safe to go out.

Wendy, John, Michael and the Lost Boys got ready to fly to London.

"Grab them!" cried Captain Hook, "Take them back to the ship!"

"Peter, help us!" cried Wendy.

At this Captain Hook was very angry. "So he's still alive! But this time I'll finish him off!"

Captain Hook crept into the
hideaway, where Peter was still
sleeping. He left a bottle of
poison on a table, wrote "Peter"
on it, then left quietly.

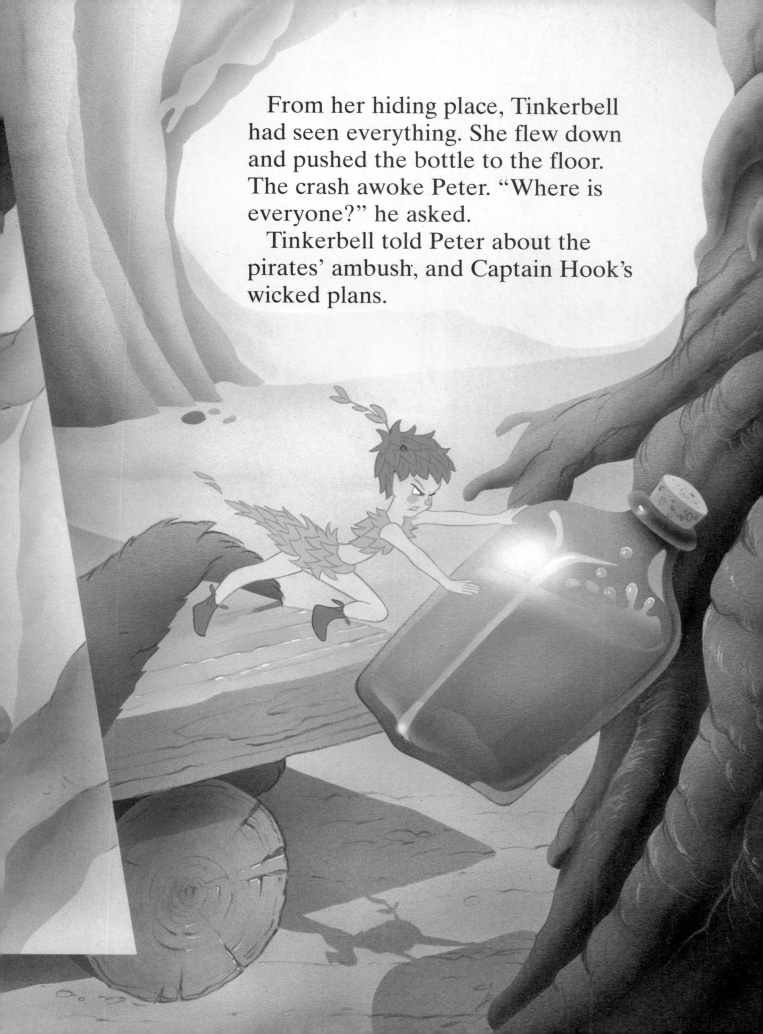

From her hiding place, Tinkerbell had seen everything. She flew down and pushed the bottle to the floor. The crash awoke Peter. "Where is everyone?" he asked.

Tinkerbell told Peter about the pirates' ambush, and Captain Hook's wicked plans.

On board the pirate ship, John and Michael were being made to walk the plank. Wendy was tied to the mast, and could do nothing to save them. Just then a strange noise came from the sea. Tick-tock, tick-tock, tick-tock. Hook went green with fear... the crocodile was back! The boys stopped at the end of the plank.

Just then Peter Pan appeared from behind the crocodile. He cut the ropes that were tied around Michael and John, then flew to release Wendy. The pirates surrounded their captain, who was almost fainting with terror. The crocodile was still waiting for his dinner!

A fierce battle began between the children and the pirates. The pirates were really rather unfit, and they soon began to get tired.

Wendy and her brothers chased the pirates around the ship. At last, tired of fighting, the pirates all jumped into the sea to escape. Meanwhile Captain Hook, who was fighting furiously with Peter, slipped and fell, straight toward the hungry crocodile!

After winning such a huge battle, Wendy wanted to go home.

"I'll take you back to London," said Peter Pan, "but I'm still going to live in Never-Never Land."

Mr. and Mrs. Darling were very surprised when their children brought the Lost Boys home, but they were happy to let them stay.

Wendy was sad to see Peter leave.

"Don't worry, Wendy!" he called. "I'll come back once a year to take you to Never-Never Land on holiday!"